Daddy Daughter Day

Daddy Daughter Day

Story by

Isabelle Bridges-Boesch

Illustrated by

Jeff Bridges

Colors and Book Design by

Rick DeLucco

DARK HORSE BOOKS

Published by Dark Horse Books
A division of Dark Horse Comics LLC
10956 SE Main Street
Milwaukie, OR 97222

DarkHorse.com
DaddyDaughterDay.com
JeffBridges.com
IsabelleBridges.com

First edition: October 2020
Ebook ISBN 978-1-50671-809-5
ISBN 978-1-50671-808-8

10 9 8 7 6 5 4 3 2 1
Printed in China

Library of Congress Cataloging-in-Publication Data

Names: Bridges, Jeff, 1949- author, illustrator. | Bridges-Boesch,
    Isabelle, author.
Title: Daddy Daughter Day / writer, Jeff Bridges, Isabelle Bridges-Boesch ;
    artist, Jeff Bridges.
Description: Milwaukie, OR : Dark Horse Books, [2020] | Audience: Ages 5+ |
    Audience: Grades K-1. | Summary: "When Belle announces to Dad that this
    day is 'Daddy Daughter Day,' it sparks a series of adventures that turns
    the house and the backyard into a clay work shop, a beauty parlor, and
    even a circus, with Mom and little brother Sammie getting involved!"–
    Provided by publisher.
Identifiers: LCCN 2020013037 | ISBN 9781506718088 (hardback) | ISBN
    9781506718095 (ebook)
Subjects: CYAC: Fathers and daughters–Fiction. | Family life–Fiction.
Classification: LCC PZ7.1.B7543 Dad 2020 | DDC [E]–dc23
LC record available at https://lccn.loc.gov/2020013037

Dedicated to
Grace & Ben

One day Belle woke up with a great idea!

Sammy's lips began to quiver & his eyebrows went like this . . .

what do you wanna do?
you pick...
...how about we play with some clay?
How about we get dressed?

Love the Red pants. I'm gonna make some dishes for Dolly.
COOL
What are you gonna make?
Hummm. I don't know. I haven't figured it out yet.

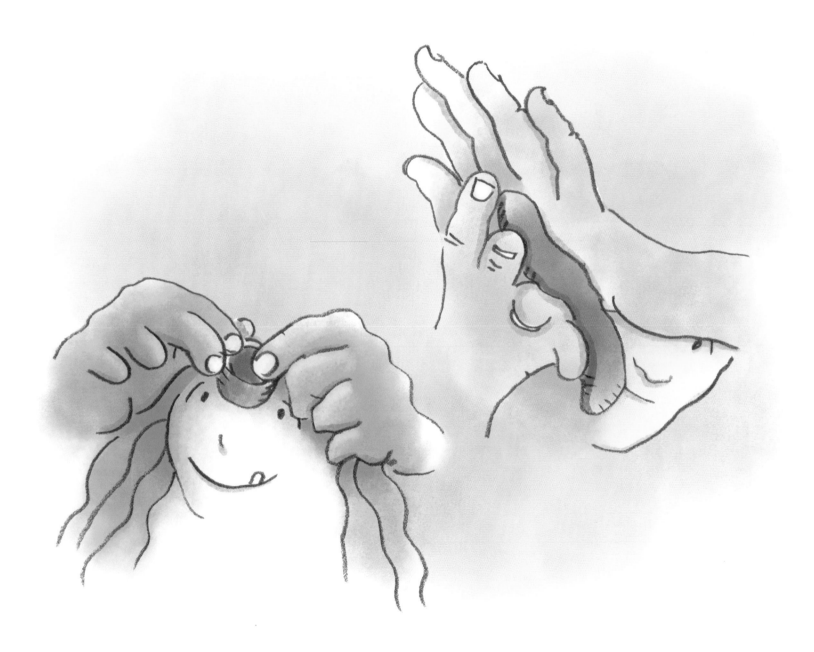

You wanna have a picnic?
IT'S my Daddy Daughter Day
Yeah... I Know ~ do You wanna have a picnic?
What'll we use for food?
We don't need real food
Yeah... I Know that
Gaaammmmy, I need your help

Stay, Sammy... You make the best mud pies Belle... I gotta go... Mom needs me

I'd be cool if it was real food.
Would it?
Yeah... 'cause I'm kind of hungry... & tired
Tired...? Well... let's rest. Hey... maybe... Daddy Daughter Day has a nap-time part
NAPTIME PART?
Yeah... you know...

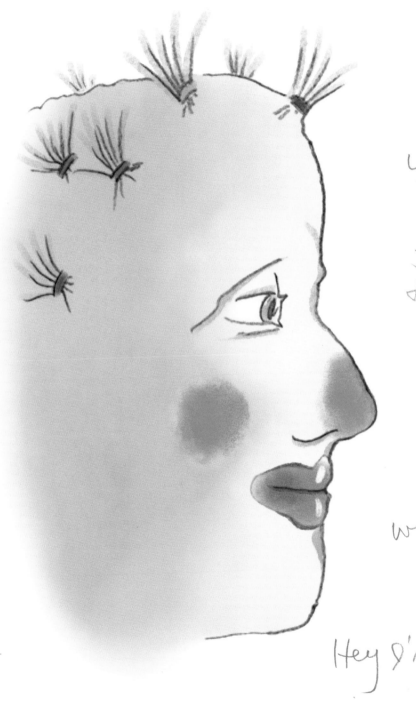

Perfect timing
yeah . . .
we better wash
our hands
you're just full
of good ideas . . .
like Daddy
Daughter Day -
what a great
Holiday!
Daddy?
yeah?
I miss you
when you're gone.
I miss you
then, too, Belle

Hey I've got a cool IDEA

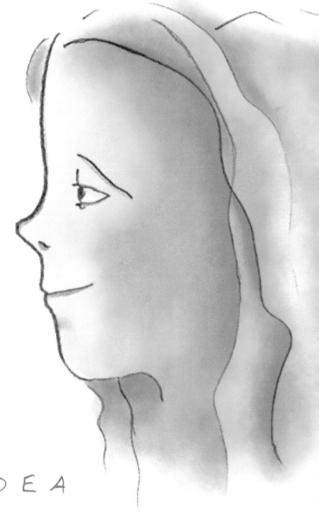

yeah ?
after dinner,
after you tuck
me in and
I'm asleep.
let's meet at our

Dreaming Tree

It's a deal
& Daddy...
yeah ?
I think you
ought to wash
your face, too,
you're looking kind of WEIRD

after Belle & Daddy shared
the Grass Rock Soup they made...

...after they ate the delicious
dinner that Sammy & Mommy made...

... After Daddy tucked Belle in,
Sang Belle her favorite lullaby*
& kissed her good night ...

... It was Daddy's bedtime ...

and time
for the last
ADVENTURE of ...

* Hear this lullaby @ daddydaughterday.com

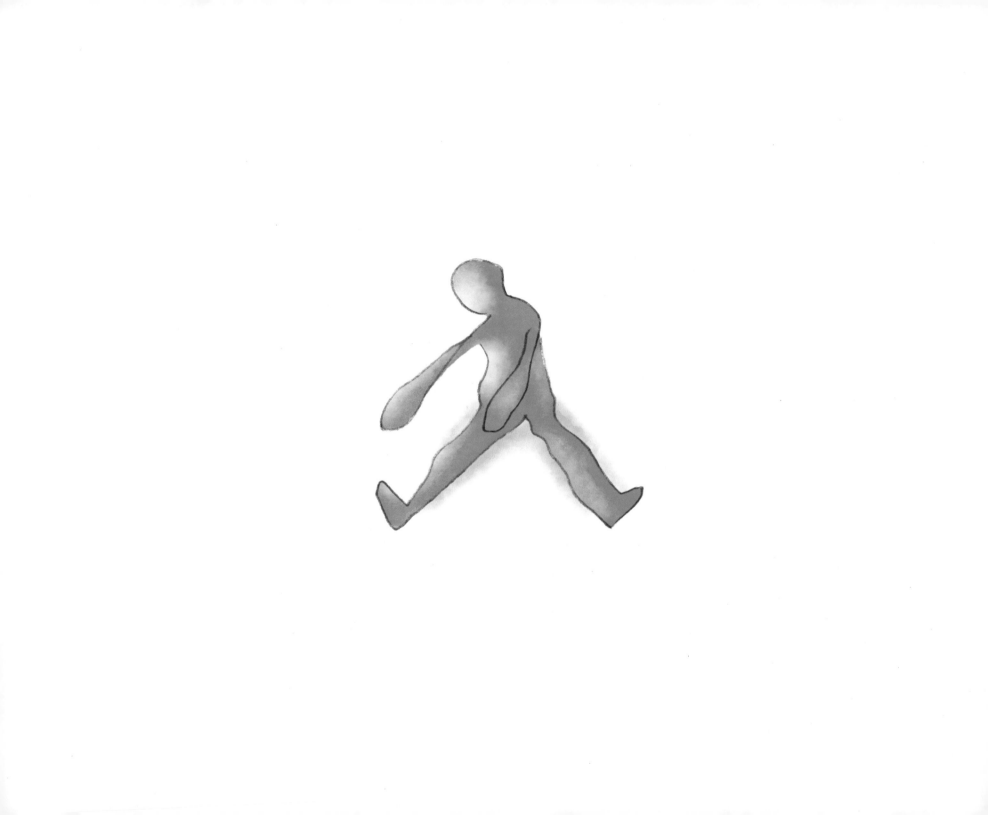

Jeff Bridges

To a generation of filmgoers, he is known as "the Dude." But to a more important group of people, he is "Dad." In addition to his film and television career, Jeff is a musician who tours with his band, the Abiders. He is a photographer and activist promoting awareness on environmental issues, including with the documentary *Living in the Future's Past* (LivingInTheFuturesPastFilm.com). He is the national spokesperson for Share Our Strength's No Kid Hungry Campaign (NoKidHungry.org).

You can learn more about him at JeffBridges.com.

A portion of the proceeds from this book
will go to support **NoKidHungry.org**

Isabelle Bridges-Boesch

Isabelle is a change maker who is committed to making meaningful contributions that create a positive impact in this world by redesigning what it means to be a mom. She is on a mission to support mothers in finding the passions and purpose that will make their hearts sing while still being great mothers.

You can learn more about her at IsabelleBridges.com.

DaddyDaughterDay.com

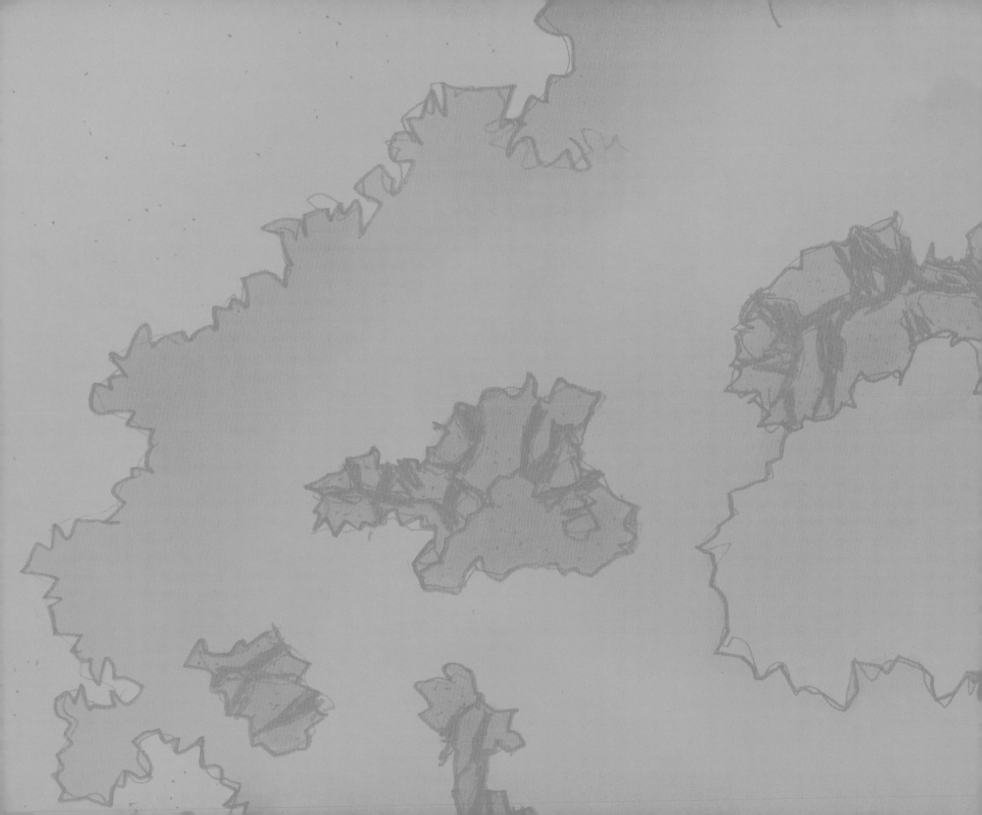